Remedies

❋

Julia Blackburn

Hazel Press

First published in 2025
by Hazel Press, 22 Coneygar Close, Bridport, Dorset DT6 3AR
www.hazelpress.co.uk

A CIP record for this title is available from the British Library

9th-century remedies adapted from: *Bald's Book of Leechdom, Wort Cunning and
Starcraft of Early England: being a collection of documents, for the most part never before printed,
illustrating the history of science in this country before the Norman Conquest. Leechdoms,
Wortcunning and Starcraft of Early England* (Cockayne Vol II 1864, Vol III 1866).

Design/typography: Dale Tomlinson
Typeface: Mrs Eaves (designed by Zuzana Licko)
Cover image: *Initial D: A Nun Feeding a Leper in Bed* in a Psalter, about 1275–1300,
unknown artist, made in Engelberg, Switzerland. The J. Paul Getty Museum,
Ms. Ludwig VIII 3 (83.MK.94), fol. 43.

ISBN 978-1-7394218-9-2

First Edition

*Printed in England by Anglia Print Ltd, Beccles, Suffolk, on 100% recycled paper,
using vegetable-based inks. Anglia Print has gained the following certifications:*

Contents

Foreword

The 6th-century physician Alexander of Tralles said that his patients — like besieged cities — must be defended by anything that gave them the courage to go on living. He found that images, amulets and all sorts of strange remedies seemed to help, even though there was no rational reason for this to be so.

As a cure for epilepsy, he recommended taking a nail from a wrecked ship:

> *make it into a bracelet*
> *and set therein the bone of a stag's heart*
> *taken from its body while alive*
> *put it on the left arm*
> *and you will be astonished by the result.*

In times when medicines did not have much to offer, then the mind needed to be persuaded to do a lot of the healing work. The person who is suffering from epilepsy does not need to see a real nail being turned into a bracelet, just imagining it is the crucial step towards recovery.

The Old English remedies included in this little collection were first written down in a 9th-century manuscript known as *Bald's Leechbook*, but their origin goes much further back. I have added my own invented remedies, that might or might not help if you are faced with sadness or fear, the loss of a friend, or the wish to be closer to a lover.

JULIA BLACKBURN

5

A blackberry bush growing by your door
protects you from Nightwalkers
because they will stop to count the berries
until dawn comes.

To cure a fever
take a snail
and make from it a clean foam
and mix with woman's milk
then drink it.
You will soon be well.

If an old lover appears before you
take him in your arms and hold him tight
until the impression of presence
becomes the fact of absence
or the fact of absence
becomes the impression of presence.
(JB)

To prevent conception
let the woman remove the testicles from a live weasel
(causing no damage to the weasel)
and let her carry the testicles in her bosom
tied in the skin of a goose
and she will not conceive.

For bringing on the menses
massage is helpful
And so is coitus.
If the woman is without fever
let her eat leeks, onions, pepper, garlic
cinnamon and scaly fish.
Let her drink strong wine.

For a husband who has become distant
make an oil scented with lavender
warm in your hands
and rub the oil between his shoulders
while he sleeps
and he will wake and turn to you.
This same can be applied to a wife
by her husband.
(JB)

For a woman about to give birth
the white substance found in the dung of eagles
when given as a drink
is advantageous
likewise the dung of baby birds
found in a swallow's nest.
Washings of this dung are useful
for many other purposes.

For sadness that cannot be spoken
take it outside at night
hide it in a quiet place
and forget where it is hidden.
(JB)

In case a man is insane
take the skin of a porpoise
and make a whip of it.
Beat the man with the whip
and he will soon be better.

Against anger
gargle with sea water
as salty as can be.
If you swallow
any of the water
your anger will return
stronger than before.
(JB)

Against nostalgia
burn wormwood
as dry or as green as you may have it
in Oil of Extreme Unction
until the third part is boiled up.
Smear over the body at a fire
and the nostalgia will be gone.

If a dream frightens you
write it on a piece of paper
and burn the paper
so the flames destroy
the memory of the dream.
It will not come to you again.
(JB)

For claiming a swarm of bees
take some earth
sprinkle it with your right hand
under your left foot
and say,
'I hold it under foot!
I have found it!'

If you spend a night
in the house of a friend
who has died
leave the window open
even in winter
and your friend will appear
just for a moment
to say goodbye.
(JB)

In case a woman suddenly turns dumb
take pennyroyal and rub it to dust
wind it in wool
lay it under the woman
it will soon be well with her.

If you miss your children
because they are far away
and busy with their own lives
sing the songs you once sang to them
and your children will seem to be close by
even though you cannot see their faces.
(JB)

If you dream of toads
it is a good dream
because toads
can protect us
from every sort of harm.
If you kill a toad
you will have misfortune
for at least a year.
(JB)

For joint pain
take dove's dung and a goat's turd
dry them thoroughly and rub to dust
mingle with honey and butter
smear the joints with the mixture
the pain will soon depart.

For aching limbs
almond oil is good
when rubbed into the skin,
so too is coitus
but only with the person you love.
(JB)

For toothache
lie face down on a ploughed field
and the toothache will take root
in the earth.
(JB)

In case a poisonous spider should bite a man
cut three incisions close to
and running away from
the wound
and let the blood flow into
a green hazel-wood spoon.
Throw the spoon away over the road
and there will be no injury.

For fear of the dark
go out at night and hide under a bush
until you have become
part of the darkness.
(JB)

For fear of the human race
think of ants
which are more numerous than we are
and will be here
long after we have gone.
(JB)

If memories fly around your head
like flocks of birds
in the evening
do not be afraid of them
and they will soon depart.
(JB)

For an itching rash
take goosefat, elecampane,
viper's bugloss, bishop's wort and cleavers
pound together well
add a spoonful of soap
a little oil
and mix thoroughly
lather it on at night
and scratch the neck after sunset
and gently pour the blood into running water
and spit three times upon it saying
'take this disease and depart with it!'
go back to your house by an open road
and go in silence.

If a man's head-pan or skull be seemingly iron-bound
lay the man flat with face upwards
drive two stakes into the ground at the armpits
lay a plank across his feet
and strike it three times with a sledge beetle
the skull will soon come right.

For sadness
walk with fast steps
around the trunk of an old tree
until you are dizzy
and your sadness will be gone
at least for now.
(JB)

For fear of flood, fire and famine
think of the enormity of the past
and sing this charm,
Cryptozoic, Palaeozoic, Jurassic,
Eocene, Oligocene, Miocene,
Pliocene, Holocene
and your fear will be gone.
(JB)

Against a gang-way weaving spider
take a hen's egg
and rub it raw into ale and a new sheep's turd
so the patient knows it not.
Give him a good cupful to drink.

For loneliness
observe a snail
also that little spider called a harvester
both of them know loneliness very well.
(JB)

For adder's bite
take common or dwarf elder
and before you cut it
hold it in your hand and say three times
'I charm and overcome all wild beasts!'
Cut the elder into three parts
with a very sharp knife
and imagine the person you wish to cure.
As you do this
take the plant and pound it
and lay it to the bite
and he will shortly be well.

To protect yourself from forgetfulness
balance on one leg
and say, 'forgetting
is also an act of memory.'
Do this as often as is necessary
especially first thing in the morning.
(JB)

If a butterfly settles on your hand
you will be wealthy.
If a robin enters your house
you will have good fortune.
If a fox accompanies you through the streets
you will find true love.
Do not entice the fox with old bones.
(JB)